The Perfect Present

Written by Marcia Vaughan

Illustrated by Kim Harley

Chapter 1

Sam had been absorbed in his painting all morning. Now he took a step back and admired his work. His satisfaction spread into a smile. His hard work had paid off!

"What are you up to Sam?" asked Mum, peering over his shoulder.

"Painting a portrait of dad," replied Sam. "What do you think?"

"Oh, Sam!" gasped Mum. "It's wonderful! How did you get it to look so like him?"

"Well," explained Sam proudly. "I sketched him last night when he was reading the paper. He was grinning at something so he had all these smiley lines on his face. Then I used the sketch to help me paint his portrait. Our teacher showed us how to make faces look lifelike by adding shadows around the eyes and nose."

Mum hugged Sam tightly and ruffled his curly hair.

"Dad will love this," she said. "It'll make a perfect birthday present."

Just as Sam was adding a bit of sparkle to dad's eyes, Molly came up behind him and snatched the painting from its stand.

"What's this?" she sneered. "Dad's birthday present, I suppose."

Sam nodded shyly. His sister was always making fun of his paintings.

"Honestly Sam, can't you think of something more original? You give Dad a picture every year! Why don't you get him a real present, like a tie or a tennis racket or something useful?"

Sam looked crushed. "But I always give dad a painting."

"Exactly!" Molly mocked. "How boring!"

Then she leaned closer to Sam and whispered in his ear,
"And do you know what Dad does with all your stupid
paintings?"

"What?"

"He chucks them away."

"No he doesn't!" cried Sam.

"Oh, yes, he does! What else do you think happened to the
pictures you gave him for Christmas and Father's Day?"

Sam's eyes began to sting. His stomach tied itself up in knots.

Suddenly his painting didn't look so special any more. It looked silly. Fighting off tears, he grabbed the portrait, scrunched it up into a ball and threw it in the bin.

Chapter 2

Later on, Sam spotted his friend, Gina, outside on her hands and knees in the dirt. Gina was fascinated by fossils, and was always digging things up.

"Hi, Gina," Sam called. "It's my dad's birthday tomorrow. What did you give your dad this year?"

"We went to the Natural History Museum for the day and I got him a brontosaurus tie. It says I DIG BONES on it. He wears it to work every day."

"Wow," sighed Sam. A tie sounded a whole lot more useful than a painting.

Sam kicked at stones as he
walked towards the park. PJ was
playing on the tyre swing.

"Hey, PJ!" he said. "What did you give your dad for
his birthday?"

PJ swung down and landed with a thud. "I got him a
model spaceship. It has over five hundred pieces. He loves it
so much he's still working on it!"

"Sounds great," said Sam, booting a big pebble into the
duck pond.

Sam walked on past the skate ramp, where he saw Kim wrestling with her kite. "Hey, Kim! Any ideas about what I should get my dad for his birthday?"

"I got my dad a chemistry set," said Kim. "He got a real blast out of it!"

"Cool!" said Sam. And all he had ever given his dad were paintings.

Sam turned and headed for home, dragging his brick-heavy feet. He really enjoyed painting, and everyone was always telling him how good he was at art. Now he didn't feel so special anymore. He wished he'd saved his pocket money so that he could buy his dad a proper present.

When Sam got home, he reluctantly fished the portrait of dad out of the bin. A lump formed in his throat.

"What's up, Sam?" called Mum from the kitchen.

"I don't have anything to give Dad for his birthday," Sam sniffed. "I can't give him this useless painting. I do that every year!"

"But Sam, this portrait is the best piece of art you've ever done. You can't throw it away!"

Sam looked closely at the crumpled, half-finished portrait. It really was a good likeness. Somehow the crinkles in the paper made it look even more realistic. He took it up to his room and set it on the stand. What was it his teacher had told him about bringing a portrait to life? He delicately dabbed more colour into the eyes and added a slight texture to the hair.

Finally, he made a frame for the portrait, then signed his name at the bottom with a flourish, the way real artists do. He hoped the paint would be dry by morning.

Chapter 3

At breakfast, Molly presented dad with a Milton Rangers football shirt and Mum gave him a gizmo for washing golf balls.

"Thanks guys," Dad grinned. "These are great presents!"

"Don't you have anything for Dad?" said Molly.

Sam stared into his cornflakes. "Only this," he said, dragging the portrait out from under the table.

His dad unwrapped the picture and studied it. He held it for a long, long time. He didn't say a word. Sam's cornflakes went soggy. He felt tears swimming up into his eyes, but when he finally looked up, Dad's face was crinkled all over with smiley lines.

"I love it, Sam! I love this painting. You must have worked very hard on it. I'm really proud of you."

Molly craned over to see the picture. "Gosh, Sam," she cried in surprise. "That really is good! Maybe you could do one of me, some time?"

Sam turned to Dad and took a deep breath. "Are you going to bin this one like all the others?"

Dad looked stunned. "What? Of course not!"

"Come with me, Sam," said Dad when breakfast was over. "I'd like to show you a very special art gallery I know."

Sam and his dad walked up the street and through the park. Eventually they came to a tall, red-brick building. Sam's dad tapped in the alarm code and pushed the door open. "This is where I work," he explained.

Sam followed his dad down a long corridor and up two
flights of stairs. When his dad finally opened the door to his
office, Sam couldn't believe his eyes. The walls were covered
with paintings...his paintings! Every picture he had ever
drawn for his dad was there, even the scribbly ones he'd
done as a baby and the splodgy hand prints from his first
day at school.

"Wow!" said Sam. "You kept all my artwork!"

"Of course I did, Sam! I love your paintings and drawings.
They make me think of you and how much I love you.
You're a very talented artist. I like to show off your pictures
to all the people who come here – it makes me so proud!
Now, where shall we hang my portrait?"

"Right there!" Sam grinned, pointing to a spot above the door.

"You know, Sam," said Dad. "This is the best birthday present a dad could ask for."